T0197454

Layla the Ladybug - Bullying

Darlington Johnson

AuthorHouse™
1663 Liberty Drive
Bloomington, IN 47403
www.authorhouse.com
Phone: 1 (800) 839-8640

Because of the dynamic nature of the Internet, any web addresses or links contained in this book may have changed
since publication and may no longer be valid. The views expressed in this work are solely those of the author and do not
necessarily reflect the views of the publisher, and the publisher hereby disclaims any responsibility for them.

Any people depicted in stock imagery provided by Thinkstock are models,
and such images are being used for illustrative purposes only.
Certain stock imagery © Thinkstock.

This book is printed on acid-free paper.

ISBN: 978-1-4520-5332-5 (sc)
ISBN: 978-1-5049-7819-4 (hc)
ISBN: 978-1-4817-0116-7 (e)

Library of Congress Control Number: 2010911368

Print information available on the last page.

Published by AuthorHouse: 09/18/2019

authorHOUSE®

This is a message to every child all over the world, remember to feel great about yourself. Try your best to overlook any negative remarks.

"Hi," my name is Layla, and I am a ladybug. I do not look like the other ladybugs. This makes me feel sad.

The other ladybugs laugh at me because of the way my body looks. I try to ignore them, and it is not easy.

My mom says, "I am beautiful and unique." I should be proud. She also says that one day, the other ladybugs are going to get used to the way I look and will leave me alone.

I began to wonder if I'm going to stay this way for the rest of my life. I hope this does not happen.

Then I got an idea! I need something that could make me look better. Is there something I can use to improve my spots?

I decided to paint my body with round black spots. "I hope the other ladybugs like it."

The next day, I started receiving compliments from the other ladybugs. I enjoyed all the positive attention.

Later that day, I walked down a street. A car splashed water on me. "OH NO!" My new spots started to disappear. This is not good. I have no more paint!

That same day, I came home dripping wet. When my mom saw me enter the front door, she looked very concerned.

I could tell my mom was very disappointed in me for painting myself. I do not blame her. I was upset with myself as well.

She told me again, I am beautiful the way I am, and I should not change myself based on what others say. Now I know I should not change myself because of anyone else's opinion.

Going forward, I will not care what negative people say. I will turn my antenna the other way. "I am proud of my appearance and myself."

Remember when people try to bully you, it is because they want to feel superior. Show them you feel fantastic about yourself. Their unkind words are meaningless to you. Sooner or later, they will move on.

Summary of Inspiration

I was inspired to write this book when I started to notice many kids not feeling good about themselves, because of negative peer pressure/ bullying. Sometimes kids can be mean to other kids. This is when we should focus on loving ourselves and ignoring the negative, challenging situations that may come our way. Layla the ladybug is another example on how we should handle the negative remarks from our peers. Just "smile", and let it go in one ear and out the other.

Darlington Johnson: Layla the Ladybug

Biography

Have you ever felt sad because of another person's negative comments about you? Most of us have experienced this. Darlington has learned to ignore the negative people and surround herself with positive people. It's how you handle certain situations that can make you the better person.

Darlington was born on February 21, 1997 in Southfield, Michigan. She is an only child. At the age of five Darlington and her mother moved to Texas. Darlington has three step-sisters, one brother, and a little dog named Pooh Bear. In her spare time she enjoys writing, reading, playing basketball, and drawing. Throughout her life, Darlington's family, God-Father, and close friends always encouraged Darlington to excel and to never give up on her dreams. Darlington also encourages others to do this as well.

Today, Darlington wants to encourage as many kids as possible to love themselves and push on in a positive way, no matter how uncomfortable a situation may appear. Positive people can be very helpful when you get that feeling of discouragement. Darlington would like for kids to remember: Positive kids can lead to a positive childhood.

Printed in the United States
By Bookmasters